In loving memory of my mother,
Lorayne Coombs   —A. J.

For Cory, Morgan, Abby,
and Gatsby —K. F.

Henry Holt and Company, LLC
Publishers since 1866
115 West 18th Street
New York, New York 10011

Henry Holt is a registered trademark
of Henry Holt and Company, LLC

Library of Congress Cataloging-in-Publication Data
Jackson, Alison.
If the shoe fits / by Alison Jackson; illustrated by Karla Firehammer.
Summary: The old woman who lives in a shoe sets out to find a larger
home for her many children, and gets mixed up in other nursery
rhymes along the way.
[1. Home—Fiction. 2. Characters in literature—Fiction. 3. Stories
in rhyme.] I. Firehammer, Karla, ill. II. Title.
PZ8.3.J13435 Im 2001   [E]—dc21   00-44858

ISBN 0-8050-6466-4
First Edition—2001 / Book design by David Caplan
Printed in the United States of America on acid-free paper. ∞
10 9 8 7 6 5 4 3 2 1

The artist used acrylic on illustration board
to create the illustrations for this book.

If the Shoe Fits

written by
Alison Jackson

illustrated by
Karla Firehammer

HENRY HOLT AND COMPANY

NEW YORK

There was an old woman who lived in a shoe.
She had so many children, she didn't know what to do.
She gave them some broth without any bread,
Then took them to live in a new home instead.

She left the old shoe to reside in a hat,

Which she shortly discovered they shared with a cat.

The cat played a fiddle from morning to night,

And then danced with a spoon till they all fled in fright.

The woman then moved to a warm woolen coat,
But all of that lint sorely tickled her throat.
When Little Jack Horner stopped in for some pie,
She decided to give a new haven a try.

She huddled her children inside a green sock,
Which someone had thoughtfully hung from a clock.
But a hickory-dickory mouse scurried through,
And she fled with her broth and her family, too.

The clock just struck one as they jumped in a tub,
But three men were sitting there, rub-a-dub dub—
A butcher, a baker, a candle man, too.
So they hid in a wall. What else could they do?

The wall soon attracted the king's horses and men,
For it seemed that an egg had exploded just then.
So she called for her children and gathered them up,
Then fearfully led them to a china teacup.

When Little Miss Muffet tried taking a sip,
The old woman grew peevish and tickled her lip.
The girl dropped the teacup and ran for the door,
While the mother transported her children once more.

The family then settled inside a torn glove.
Still the children did nothing but push, yell, and shove.
When twenty-four blackbirds arrived seeking shelter,
She instructed her children to run helter-skelter.

They discovered a bowl that was empty at least.
But then King Cole grabbed it, preparing to feast.
The family escaped from that terrible house
And sought further refuge, invading a blouse.

The blouse was then seized by the good Queen of Hearts,
Who slipped it on quickly to start making tarts.
So the family slid down the seam of her sleeve
And into a jar, but would you believe . . .

The glass jar belonged to Old Mother Hubbard,
Who immediately snatched it to put in her cupboard.
But the woman and children did manage to rock it.
The jar overturned, and they fell in a pocket.

The pocket was part of a red satin vest,
Which the Grand Duke of York wore while puffing his chest.
He puffed it so full they were squeezed from his suit
And landed one by one in his black leather boot.

Now the boot was too small for a family this size,
But the woman had grown much more patient and wise.
"If the shoe fits, then wear it," she said to her clan.
And she led them right back where this story began.

She was still an old woman who lived in a shoe.
And she still had those children, but she knew what to do.
She gave them some broth and kissed all their faces,
Then tucked them in bed and tied up the laces.